Lessons Learned

"Tea Party" -- What if the first time your best friend drags you to a FemDom "Tea Party" you see your former boyfriend serving canapes naked?

"Blind Date" -- How do you respond when you find your ex-husband hanging out at the restaurant where you planned to meet your "Blind Date"?

"To Serve" -- If you love a vanilla woman and you only want "To Serve," how do you introduce her to the lifestyle without scaring her away?

"Change in View" -- What if a "Change in View" alters the attitude of the man you mentored so he could find his perfect Mistress?

I.G. Frederick trades words for cash, specializing in erotic fiction and poetry since 2001. Her erotic short stories appear in Hustler Fantasies, Forum, Foreplay, and Desire Presents, as well as electronic, audio, and print anthologies. Her novels receive high praise from readers, critics, and other authors.

A FemDom, Ms. Frederick, owns the man she adores. Although dominant in the rest of his life, he demonstrates his love by serving as her submissive. Ms. Frederick often writes about finding love in BDSM relationships from the authority of one enjoying that for almost a decade.

http://eroticawriter.net/

Sometimes you need
more than love ...

Lessons
Learned

Four FemDom

Love Stories

I.G. Frederick
Author of Dommemoir & Cougar Conquests

Lessons Learned
© **2014 by I.G. Frederick**

ISBN: 978-1937471-17-0

Pussy Cat Press
http://pussycatpress.com/publisher.html/
P.O. Box 19764
Portland OR 97280

First published electronically in 2011

Table of Contents

Tea Party

By I.G. Frederick

Lynette watched her waist curve in slightly and her tits push up when Theresa pulled on the laces of the leather corset.

"Is that too tight?"

Lynette put her hands against the firm leather covering her from just above her areola to below the top of her hips and sucked air into her lungs. "I can still breathe. Barely."

"Perfect." Theresa smiled and tied the long laces into an attractive bow. "You'll have them all groveling at your feet."

Lynette laughed and fluffed up her short auburn curls with her fingers. "I thought that was the point of this event."

Theresa wound her long own blond hair into an elegant French twist and pinned it with black feathers and rhinestones. She wore a pink brocade corset that emphasized her creamy complexion and a short red skirt that showed off her long, slender legs.

Lynette frowned. Compared to her best friend, she looked awkward and chunky. Although she'd agreed to wear one of Theresa's corsets, she stuck with her own full, below-the knee skirt to disguise thunder thighs and a bit of a belly. "I don't know if I'm really cut out to be a FemDom. Maybe I should skip the tea."

"Absolutely not!" Theresa handed her a pair of spiked, four-inch heels. "You've been moping around ever since Roger broke up with you." She pulled on knee-high, black leather boots. "You need to start circulating again."

Lynette slipped her bare feet into the shoes and tried to keep her balance. "But, I'm not a FemDom."

Theresa laughed. "You're single because you *are* a Fem-Dom and vanilla relationships won't work for you." She grabbed the handle of a black, leather, rolling case and pulled it toward the apartment door. "You need a guy who'll do what you tell him and thank you for the privilege."

Lynette scowled, but locked the door and followed Theresa down the hallway to the elevator, bracing her hands on the walls to keep her balance. By the time they reached the parking garage under the building, she'd gotten the hang of walking in the high heels and enjoyed the sound of their footsteps clicking across the cement.

Theresa maneuvered her car onto the street and headed north on Alaskan Way. Sunday afternoon traffic was light and they made it to the Center in less than fifteen minutes. Theresa parked outside a drab, nondescript warehouse building, and led Lynette to an unmarked door, pulling the case behind her. Inside the large room, walled off from the rest of the building, sofas, arm chairs, and tables surrounded by folding chairs were arranged on one side. On the other side, three beds, a St. Andrew's cross, four massage tables, and a spanking bench filled the space.

A naked male, about six feet tall with a shaved head and a goatee, bowed when they entered. "Good afternoon, Goddesses. We're so very grateful you could join us." He handed each of them a printed menu with a list of goodies that made Lynette's mouth water.

He turned to Theresa. "Would you like me to store your toy bag over there?" He pointed to a collection of suitcases, duffle bags, and plastic tubes in one corner."

She smiled and gave him the handle.

Another male, wearing a pink French maid's outfit with full petticoats and size 13, pink, two-inch heels curtseyed. "Would you ladies prefer seating at the table or on one of the sofas?"

Theresa scanned both areas. "Sofa, please."

"Yes, Ma'am." He sashayed in the direction of the nearest sofa, which was occupied by one woman who was going over the menu options with a naked male kneeling at her feet.

She looked up when Theresa sat down next to her. "Darling, so good to see you." They did air kisses. "Who's your friend?"

"Emily, this is Lynette. It's her first time."

"Oh, excellent." Emily had a long, thick gray braided wrapped around her head and wore a black lace catsuit under a tiny black, strapless, spandex dress. "Welcome, my dear. Don't hesitate to ask any questions you might have."

Lynette smiled, but inside she was wondering how she could compete with all these hot women. The man kneeling at Emily's feet shifted. He had close cropped salt and pepper hair and wore a small black apron that barely covered his crotch. "May I bring you Goddesses some tea?" He pointed to their menus. "We have Earl Grey, Irish Breakfast, peppermint, and wild raspberry."

"Earl Grey with milk and sugar." Theresa crossed one leg over the other. The guy's apron fluttered upwards.

Lynette didn't care much for regular tea and she hated peppermint. "Wild raspberry, please."

The man scooted back, rose to his feet, bowed, and scurried off toward a door at the far end of the room. Lynette watched more women arriving and was encouraged to see not all of them looked like they'd stepped out of the pages of a fetish magazine. A couple of them made her seem thin.

Their outfits ranged from plain black blouse and skirt to full-length, red latex. The man in the apron returned carrying a tray with three china cups. He bent over in front of each of them in turn. Lynette lifted the last saucer and the aroma of brewed raspberries actually enticed her to take a sip.

Another man, naked except for a bow tie, appeared with a tray of canapés. Lynette selected a puffed pastry which she discovered had a smoked salmon filling, and a miniature, crustless, cucumber sandwich. She set both on the edge of her saucer and looked with envy at the women surrounding the table with plates in front of them for all the goodies.

Two men carried over a piece of acrylic about three feet long and two feet wide. The one man, chunky and covered with dark hair everywhere but on his head, got down on all fours in front of them and the other balanced the acrylic on his back. Emily set her cup and saucer on the "table." Bemused, Lynette did the same. Moments later, half a dozen men paraded out from the kitchen. One had a stack of plates, another a pile of napkins in one hand and a basket of forks in the other. The others carried trays of tea sandwiches, stuffed mushrooms, fruit skewers, and pinwheels with gruyere and prosciutto.

Lynette's plate slid from her fingers and landed on the carpet when she realized Roger was carrying one of the trays. "Is Ma'am all right?" The man wearing the pink French maid's outfit knelt in front of her. "Do you need a glass of water? More tea? A fan?" He extracted a white silk fan with pink cherry blossoms from his apron pocket, opened it, and waved it at Lynette.

She shook her head. "No, thank you very much. I'll be fine." She turned to Theresa. "I need to get out of here."

"Why?" She nibbled delicately on a walnut and cream cheese sandwich. "He's here for the same reason you are. You can ignore him or, if you prefer, I can lend you a cane and you can whip his miserable ass for breaking up with you."

Lynette just stared at her friend. *Who is this woman?* Roger had disappeared and French maid was refilling her cup from a flowered china tea pot. "If I may be so bold, Goddess, would you like me to fetch you a clean plate and a sampling of the delicacies we've prepared for your enjoyment this afternoon?"

She nodded, unable to find her voice. For a while she leaned back and nibbled at the wonderful treats. Everything tasted so good, she soon forgot about Roger and asked French maid to bring her another plateful.

"I'm so glad Ma'am appreciates our culinary skills. Remember, Ma'am, we've also a number of dessert selections we'll be bringing out a bit later."

Lynette took a deep breath and relaxed enough to give him a big smile. "Everything is wonderful. I just was shocked to see someone I used to know."

"Don't worry, Ma'am. What's seen in the dungeon stays in the dungeon. Everyone here knows better than to tattle on anyone else."

She giggled. *I guess Roger has a lot more to worry about in that respect than I do. At least I've got clothes on.*

After she emptied her plate and set it on the "table" Roger appeared at her elbow carrying a silver tray. "Would Ma'am care for some dessert?"

French maid handed her a clean plate and she took a lemon tart, a truffle, and a chocolate-covered strawberry from Roger's tray.

"Thank you, Ma'am. Please alert me if you'd like more." Roger scooted around to offer the tray to Theresa and Emily. Lynette bit into the strawberry and closed her eyes so she could enjoy the flavors of rich dark chocolate encasing luscious berry sweetness without distraction.

When she opened her eyes, French maid was kneeling at her elbow again, fan in his hand.

She waved him away, "I'm fine, thanks. Just enjoying these wonderful strawberries." Roger appeared out of nowhere and held the tray in front of her. "Perhaps, Ma'am would like another?"

"I think I would." Lynette added two more to her plate. She looked up into Roger's baby blue eyes and was startled to see what could have been adoration in his expression. He looked pretty good, especially compared to some of the pudgier guys. He was almost six feet of lean, muscular male with a full head of curly dark hair and another triangle of black curls surrounding his exposed and partially erect cock.

"I hope Ma'am won't be offended if I told her that she is the most beautiful woman here today. I've never seen her look so stunning."

French maid tucked his fan back into his apron pocket. "Ma'am is indeed quite beautiful. If I may be so bold, perhaps she would allow me the honor of giving her a foot massage?"

Roger dropped to his knees. "If Ma'am would like someone to worship her feet, give her a back massage, or provide her with any other attention or services, she might be inclined to remember my skills in that department." He set his tray on the "table" and leaned over and kissed the tops of Lynette's shoes.

Eyes wide, she stared, first at Roger, then at French maid and back at Roger. She picked up one of the strawberries and licked at the chocolate with the tip of her tongue.

"Ma'am, I realize we just met." French maid tried to edge closer to Lynette. Roger held his ground. "But, I'm sure Ma'am will find that I give excellent massages of feet, back, and anywhere else Ma'am might have a need." He extended his tongue and licked the tip of his nose.

Lynette bit into the strawberry. Without taking her eyes off the two men, she leaned over and whispered into Theresa's ear. "They're vying for my attention."

She felt Theresa shrug. "You don't have to choose. There's more men than women."

Chocolate and strawberry glided down Lynette's throat.

She nodded at French maid. "I'd like a shoulder and neck rub."

He stood and curtseyed. "Oh, yes, Ma'am. Thank you so very much, Ma'am." He moved behind the sofa and rubbed at the tension in her muscles until her eyes drifted half closed.

Remembering Roger, she lifted one foot and wiggled it. He eased the shoe off and kissed her foot while his fingers massaged her heel. She purred. If this was how men treated FemDoms, she needed to retract the statement she'd made to Theresa earlier. She leaned back into the sofa cushions and French maid's strong fingers. Roger covered her feet in kisses and, with his thumbs, eased away the discomfort created by wearing high heels.

She sensed Theresa leave and when she looked up she saw her friend binding the guy in the bow tie to the cross. Sweet, kind Theresa took a whip from the case she'd brought to the party and swung it back and forth, covering the man's ass and back with red marks. Lynette was too blissed out to care. Her head dropped forward onto her chest and French maid massaged her neck until she didn't think it capable of holding her head up.

Roger was working his way up her thighs, kissing first one, then the other. He seemed determined to press his lips to every inch of her legs. When he reached her knees, he lifted his head and looked up at her pleading. "Please, Goddess. It's been so very long. May I have the honor of worshiping you orally?"

Lynette opened her eyes and stared at him. "You broke up with me, remember."

He lowered his eyes. "The biggest mistake I ever made, apparently. I had no idea you were a FemDom. You never ..." He fell forward and pressed his cheek against her feet. "Please forgive me, Ma'am. I shouldn't have said anything critical. I realize I'm not worthy of your attention, but if you'd consider allowing this poor miserable male an opportunity to serve you, I'd do my very best to make up for any inadequacies in my past performance."

French maid continued massaging Lynette's neck, making it hard for her to register what Roger said. All she knew was that two males vying for her attention, strong fingers caressing her shoulders and feet, and the lingering taste of strawberries and chocolate combined to make her horny as hell. She decided to sort out things with Roger some other time and flipped her skirt over his head. He wasted no time and kissed his way up to her thighs. After covering them both with his lips, he nuzzled his way between them. French maid had shifted from massage to soft, sensuous stroking of her skin from her neck down to the top of her corset.

Lynette sighed with pleasure and spread her legs wide enough to allow Roger better access. He reached up, eased her panties aside, and ran his tongue between her lips. She'd forgotten how good he was. Now that she thought about it, she'd always been the one to pull his head from between her legs, mostly because she felt obligated to reciprocate and didn't want to spend that much time sucking him. But, according to Theresa, that's not how it worked for FemDoms.

Roger ran his tongue up and down the inside of Lynette's slit while French maid caressed her arms and licked the chocolate off her fingers. Roger found her clit with the tip of his tongue and teased it until Lynette whimpered. She wiggled further down on the sofa and draped her knees over Roger's shoulders. He pushed his tongue into her and used his nose to massage her clit. French maid sucked on first one finger and then the other. Lynette was panting. Roger clamped his lips on her clit and flicked at it with his tongue. She exploded, clamping her free hand over her mouth to keep from screaming out loud. He kept licking and sucking up all the juices pouring from her until she came again.

Exhausted, Lynette pushed Roger's head away. He kissed his way back down her thighs, then gently lifted her feet until she lay on the sofa. She wondered what had become of Emily.

"Thank you so very much, Goddess, for allowing me the

great honor of tasting and pleasuring you." Roger lay his head just below her breasts and she realized the "table" had disappeared also. She managed to pick up one hand and lay it on his head, fingering his soft curly hair. He sighed. "I've missed you."

"Why did you leave?"

He shrugged without removing his head from where it rested on the leather. "I met a FemDom online and she invited me to come serve her. We didn't click, but I discovered that I need this. To be honest, I didn't think you had it in you. I'm sorry. I should have had more faith in you."

Gradually, Lynette became aware of the surroundings that had faded from her consciousness while Roger drove her wild. Four naked men attended two women who lay face down on massage tables. Theresa had turned bow tie around and continued to whip his chest and thighs. Another man was tied to the spanking bench and Emily was swatting his ass with a big wooden paddle. The guy who'd worn the apron lay on his back on the third massage table, twenty or thirty clothes pins attached to his balls. Two of the beds were occupied. French maid had disappeared.

She pulled her fingers through Roger's curls over and over again, not quite sure what to make of it all. He'd broken her heart when he stopped calling and didn't return her texts. She'd wept for a week when he changed his relationship on Facebook to "single." Theresa's words echoed in her mind: "You need a guy who'll do what you tell him and thank you for the privilege."

"Go find me some more strawberries."

"Yes, Ma'am. Thank you, Ma'am." Roger rose to his feet and headed to the kitchen.

He was gone so long, Lynette almost fell asleep in post orgasmic euphoria. She opened her eyes when she sensed someone kneeling beside her.

"I'm so very, very sorry, Ma'am. It appears all the strawberries are gone. I found the last three truffles, or if you prefer

I can get dressed and go find some strawberries."

She opened her eyes. He knelt in front of her holding out a plate, a worried look on his face and his cock pointing straight at her. She opened her mouth and he lifted one truffle, holding it so she could take a bite. Amaretto and chocolate melted in her mouth. She smiled.

"Oh, I'm so grateful that you like it, Ma'am." He offered her the other half. When he presented her another one, she shook her head. "You have a bit of chocolate on your mouth, Ma'am. May I clean it off for you?" When she nodded, he licked around her mouth which started her panting again. She put one hand on the back of his head and kissed him hard, thrusting her tongue into his mouth. He closed his eyes and parted his lips, welcoming her and getting her all hot and bothered again.

Lynette swung her legs off the sofa and sat up. She looked around for her shoes. "Did Ma'am want these?" Roger extracted them from underneath the sofa. When she nodded, he kissed each foot and slipped them on. She held up one hand and he stood to help her to her feet. Grabbing his earlobe, she wobbled over to the empty bed. On the way, she noticed a green plastic bowl full of condoms. "Get some of those."

"Oh, yes, Ma'am." When she released his ear, Roger grabbed a handful of packets and followed her. The mattress was bare with a clean, folded sheet in one corner. Roger deposited the condoms in her hands and opened the sheet, spreading it across the bed and tucking the corners under the mattress.

When he turned to face her, Lynette pushed one finger into his chest. He fell onto his back. She looked over at the guy with the clothes pins. The woman in red latex was whipping his cock with a metal whisk. Turning back to Roger, she stood there for a moment with one eyebrow raised. *Need to learn more about that sort of thing.* But his rigid cock beckoned her and she couldn't resist its call. She let the condom packages sift through her fingers to land on Roger's chest and waited while he extracted one and put it on.

Climbing onto the bed, Lynette lifted her skirt just high enough to throw one leg over his hips. She reached under it to guide his cock into her and sighed with pleasure when it slid inside. Unfortunately, she wasn't sure what to do at that point. The corset made it impossible for her to move in this position. "Make me come again."

"Oh, yes, Ma'am. Thank you, Ma'am." He pulled his knees up and, with one hand on each leather-encased hip, pushed up into her and dropped back on the bed, repeating the movement until her breath came in short gasps. She removed one of his hands and shoved it under her skirt. He continued thrusting, and found her clit with his thumb, massaging it until she trembled and cried out.

"Ladies!" French maid stood in the middle of the room. "I'm so very sorry to interrupt all your fun, but we unworthy males have to stop serving you now so we can clean up this space for the next event. We hope you all have found some small pleasure in our attentions and that you'll return next month and let us worship you again." He spoke to the group, but he stared at Lynette.

She pushed herself off Roger, extracted herself from the bed, and managed to compose herself enough to walk over to where Theresa was zipping closed her case.

"Have fun?"

Lynette grinned. "I think I like this FemDom stuff." She could see Roger stripping the sheet off the bed and carrying it to a hamper in the corner. His cock still stuck straight out, covered in a pink condom. It felt at once awkward and vengeful to walk away from him utterly satisfied knowing he'd gotten no release.

French maid knelt before her and kissed first one foot and then the other. "Thank you so much, Goddess, for allowing this unworthy wretch to serve you this afternoon. I very much hope you'll return next month."

"I very much enjoyed your attentions." Lynette patted him on his head. "I believe I will."

When she turned toward the door, she saw Emily sliding her arms into a black trench coat held for her by the "table." "Lovely meeting you, my dear. Next time we'll have to chit chat more and get to know one another better."

Lynette smiled. "I'd like that. I enjoyed this afternoon a lot."

While Theresa drove back to the apartment, Lynette turned her phone back on and found three text messages from Roger.

"Beloved Goddess, thank you so very much for allowing me the honor of pleasuring you this afternoon. Can't begin to express how grateful I am."

"I hope you'll consider forgiving this stupid male for past transgressions and allow him to earn the privilege of groveling at your feet."

"I promise, if you'll only give me another opportunity, I'll spend every moment I can serving you in any way you choose. Love, Roger."

Stunned, she just stared at the phone in her hand.

"I take it you've heard from Roger?" Theresa turned onto Alaskan Way.

Lynette raised one eyebrow above the other. "You knew he'd be there."

Theresa laughed. "Of course. He started coming a couple of months after he broke up with you. I'd gotten so tired of you moping around since he left, at the last tea I decided to have a heart to heart with him. He really does love you, Lynette." She pulled into the parking garage. "He just couldn't figure out how to explain that he needed you to take control of him and, for that matter, beat him regularly."

She turned off the engine and turned sideways in her seat. "You've gotten a taste. If you're serious about going down this path, I can mentor you and there's classes at the Center you can take."

Lynette grinned. She responded to Roger's last text: "I'll think about it." She showed the message to Theresa before she pressed send.

Theresa laughed. "Something tells me you'll be a quick study."

Blind Date

By I.G. Frederick

Trish glanced around the restaurant, but didn't see anyone resembling the man who'd corresponded with Eastside-Domme. Instead, much to her dismay, she spotted her ex-husband hunched over his Blackberry in the far corner of the main dining room. Disgusted, she stepped to one side of the host stand, out of his line of sight.

"Are you meeting someone, Ma'am?" The perky blonde startled her, but Trish kept her composure.

"Yes, but he's not here yet. Can you seat me over there?" She pointed to the dining area on the other side of the L-shaped restaurant. "I'd like to sit near the fireplace."

The blonde looked at her watch. "That section's supposed to close in half an hour and the fire's not lit this time of year."

Trish shrugged. "I could just leave." If she waited outside for geeksub07, they could go into the bar, which had a separate entrance.

"Ma'am, I'd be happy to seat you back there, but you'll get spotty service 'cause we'll only have one other girl working."

Trish smiled. "No problem." She followed the blonde, admiring her slender figure and long slim legs, to a table in the back corner where she could still see the front entrance, but was hidden from the other seating area and her ex. The light was dimmer on this side as well, more flattering. She'd warned geeksub07 she was a BBW, and he assured her that was his thing. But, everyone seemed to have a different definition of what that meant.

Trish ordered a glass of Chablis to calm her nerves and give her something to do with her hands while she waited. In the fifteen months since her divorce, she'd learned a lot about what she wanted in a man and a relationship. But, she still hadn't found anyone attractive who was interested in serving a short, plump, over-forty Domme.

Every time the bells above the restaurant front door tinkled, Trish looked up. She smiled at every man who entered alone, but none even glanced her way. Although she sipped slowly, her glass was empty and she still sat alone. She slid toward the edge of the booth to leave, but then grabbed the menu to hold it in front of her face when she saw Brian paying his bill at the host stand.

"Hey, Trish."

She lowered the menu and looked up. He still looked good with just a touch of grey at the temples of his wavy black hair and no wrinkles around his soulful brown eyes. "Watcha doing here?"

She set the menu down and rose to her feet. "Getting stood up, apparently." The top of her head, barely came up to his shoulder. While he was lean and muscular, she had, well, curves if you wanted to be polite, flab if you didn't. The differences had earned them a behind-their-back married nickname of Mutt and Jeff.

"Me, too. I didn't want to eat alone, so now I'm famished. Buy you dinner?"

She tilted her head, looking up at him, wondering what he wanted. They'd spoken fewer than a dozen times since the divorce, usually about financial matters that still required both their signatures.

"I guess." She sat back down. *At least the evening won't be a total waste.*

"You look really nice." Brian slid into the booth across from her and smoothed the red and white checkered, vinyl table-cloth with his palms.

Too bad I wasted my effort. "Thanks," she said aloud. Trish had worn an extra-large, low-cut black blouse that empha-sized her cleavage and a flowing black skirt that hid her belly.

"Excuse me, Miss?" Brian waved at the waitress who was walking from the bar area to the kitchen door behind Trish. "We'd like to order dinner."

"I'll send someone over," she said and disappeared.

"What've you been up to?"

Trish picked up the menu and squinted at the small print in the dim light, debating between a healthy salad or the fish and chips she really had a taste for. The perky blonde stood in front of the table. She looked at Brian, looked at Trish, then pulled a pen from behind her ear and smiled. "What can I get you two?"

"I'll have the fish and chips, extra tartar sauce, and an-other glass of wine."

"Bring me a bacon double cheeseburger with fries."

"Will that be one check or two."

"Two." "One." They said at the same time, then both laughed.

"I said I'd buy, remember?"

Trish nodded. The waitress disappeared.

"You never answered my question."

She shrugged. "Let's just say, I've been getting to know myself better."

"And, looking for love?" He waved his hand across the table. "I assume you were stood up by a blind date?"

She nodded. "You, too?"

He held up his phone. "She wouldn't give me her phone

number." He scowled. "I sent her three e-mails since I arrived, but nothing."

It had never occurred to Trish to use her phone to check her e-mail. She dug it out of her purse and discovered three messages from geeksub07. She read the first one and her eyes widened. "At the restaurant you selected. In the corner of main dining room to right of entrance." Her jaw dropped when she saw the second. "I need to stay out of sight. My ex-wife just showed up. Fortunately, she's in the other room."

She looked up at Brian. "You're geeksub07?"

His own mouth fell open and he stared at her, eyes as wide as hers. After several attempts at getting his mouth to form words, he managed to whisper, "EastsideDomme?"

She nodded and the blonde chose that moment to set their plates in front of them. Trish dipped a fry into tartar sauce and bit off the coated end. When the blonde was out of earshot, she stuck the rest back in the paper container and exhaled. "When did you decide you wanted to be a submissive?" All the correspondence they'd exchanged suddenly took on new meaning as she correlated what she knew about the man with what he had written. She broke off one end of a piece of fish with her fork and brought the steaming morsel close enough to her lips to blow on.

"Probably when I was in college." He picked up his burger and took a bite.

Trish dropped her fork back onto her plate, the fish uneaten, and stared at him.

"Part of what I found attractive about you in the first place, Trish, was your assertiveness at work and the way you always took control of the situation when you volunteered." He dipped a few fries into his paper container of catsup and munched on them. "But, at home, you always asked me for advice, wanted to share in the housework. Even knowing you're EastsideDomme, I can't believe you wrote those e-mails."

Trish smiled, speared a piece of fish and ate it, relishing

the contrast of the smooth white halibut against the crunchy breading. "I wasn't looking to share the housework with you, I wanted to make sure it didn't all get dumped in my lap. And, as I said, I've put a lot of effort this past year and a half into getting a better idea of who I am and what I want." Things she had always found puzzling about her ex-husband started making sense.

She leaned forward on her elbows and stared at him. "Were you completely honest in the e-mails you wrote to EastsideDomme?"

He set his burger down, put his hands in his lap, and lowered his eyes. "Yes, Ma'am."

Trish watched him for a moment while she ate, savoring the combination of fried potato, greasy mayonnaise, and tangy pickle relish. Food tasted better when the man sitting across from you liked women with meat on their bones.

She now realized that the last years of their marriage had disintegrated into a shouting match because neither one of them was getting what they needed. If he lived up to the promises of geeksub07... "You may continue eating, boy."

"Yes, Ma'am. Thank you, Ma'am." He lifted his burger to his lips and peeked at her from downcast eyes. "Perhaps Ma'am would be more willing to answer my original question, now? What *have* you been up to?"

She laughed and squeezed the remains of the tartar sauce out of the paper container onto the few fries left. "I've taken classes at the CSPC. Read every book on the subject in the library there plus a few I bought myself. I go to the FemDom tea every month and sometimes the potlucks."

"Too funny. I spend a lot of time at the Center, too, but mostly I've been going to the bondage and pansexual play parties and, when they have it, top/bottom speed dating." He wiped his hands off on the paper napkin that had been rolled around his tableware.

"I assume you went online for the same reason I did?" She mashed the leftover bits of breading together with her fork. "Couldn't find the right one?"

"I found the right one years ago," he said softly. "If I'd only had the courage then to tell you what I wanted and needed..."

The blonde came back and picked up their empty plates. "Dessert? Special tonight's cheesecake with strawberry sauce."

Trish had a taste for more than the menu offered, but couldn't resist the described temptation. "I'll have the cheese-cake. What other desserts do you have?"

"Bread pudding, ice cream, and apple pie."

"Bring him a piece of the pie, à la mode."

Brian smiled.

She dabbed the napkin at her lips. "Have you dated any-one seriously since the divorce?"

"No, Ma'am."

"Had sex with anyone?"

"I've played with other women, Ma'am. But I've had no sexual contact with anyone for," he scowled again, "Two years."

Trish frowned. They'd started counseling two years ago, a waste of time and money.

He leaned forward and whispered. "Maybe if we'd had a better counselor, one who was kink aware..."

The blonde set their desserts in front of them along with new napkin-wrapped tableware. Trish reached over and took a spoonful of his ice cream and scooped up the point of his pie. The apples were sugary tart and the crust buttery flaky with the ice cream enveloping the combination in vanilla goodness. In contrast, the cheesecake offered creamy richness smothered in strawberries bursting with sweetness.

She nodded to Brian. "You may have the pie."

"Thank you, Ma'am."

While they savored their desserts in silence, she thought

of all the good things about their ten-year marriage. Could she get back together with him? Was he really willing to cede all control to her? Did it matter? Right now, she had the rather handsome man she had once loved ready, for the moment at least, to obey her whims. And she was horny.

When Brian scraped the last bit of pie and ice cream from his plate, Trish said: "I haven't had anyone attend to my sexual needs for two years, either." She licked another bit of cheesecake off her spoon with the tip of her tongue. "And, I don't believe I can wait any longer for that to be rectified."

Brian paled. "Here?"

She shrugged. "We're practically alone. Between the tablecloth and my full skirt, I expect you should be able to remain discreet."

He looked from the kitchen door to the one leading to the bar. "Yes, Ma'am." He slid out of sight. Moments later, his warm hands caressed her ankle and he slipped her sandal from her foot. He kissed his way across the top from her toes to her ankle then back along the bottom. Trish closed her eyes and suppressed a moan. He sucked first one, then all of her toes into his mouth and her breathing got heavier. She heard the kitchen door open and took another small bite of the little bit of cheesecake left. Whoever ventured from the kitchen to the bar, didn't acknowledge her.

Brian turned his attention to her other foot, apparently unaware of the interruption. Trish shuddered, remembering how good he was with his tongue. She opened her legs wider and pulled his face closer with the back of her free heel. Brian obediently ducked his head under her skirt and kissed his way up her meaty thighs, pushing his face in between them to her already damp panties. She rested the back of her knees on his shoulders and lifted her hips enough for him to slide the panties out of his way.

Sitting with only her skirt between her ass and the pleather seat of the booth, she hesitated. Sex in public was not on her bucket list. Still, Brian's willingness to serve her in this way was a huge turn on. She opened her legs wider and slid down enough to brace her feet on the opposite booth. He kissed his way back up the inside of her thigh until he reached her bush which he gently spread apart with his fingers. She heard him inhale deeply, then he kissed her sensitive flesh and she shuddered again. He drew his tongue up along the inside of first one thick lip and then the other and pushed it inside her. She grabbed at the bench on either side of her hips to keep from sliding further down and landing in his lap.

Finally, his lips embraced her clit and the point of his tongue against her nub sent her over the edge. She had to press her lips together to keep from calling out and she could feel herself gushing. He licked up everything and she struggled to keep from coming again and starting a vicious cycle. Releasing the bench long enough to grab one of the new napkins, she handed it to him so he could wipe off his face.

He eased her panties back into place and replaced her sandals before reemerging in his seat. "I hope that will tide Ma'am over until we get home?"

She might have scolded him for presuming she would take him home, except she had every intention of doing so. Sliding out from the booth, she straightened her skirt, grabbed her purse, and tried to wobble towards the entrance. Brian threw several bills on the table, put one arm behind her back and guided her to the door. The cooling evening air refreshed her a little once they emerged, but she still felt unsteady.

"Begging Ma'am's pardon, but I don't believe she should be driving in her current condition. If she would allow me to drive her home in her car, I could take the bus back here tomorrow to retrieve mine."

She nodded and fished out her keys. Brian helped her into the passenger side and adjusted the driver's seat all the way back before climbing in. "I realize I'm being presumptuous in assuming Ma'am would keep me overnight, but I was very much hoping she would allow me the honor of pleasuring her more and then making her breakfast in the morning." He guided the car out of the parking lot and didn't speak again until they got caught by a red light.

He turned to face her. "Trish, I swear, I never stopped loving you. I just couldn't live vanilla anymore. I dropped hints, but I was afraid to just come right out and tell you..." The light turned green and he pulled forward. "I hope Ma'am will allow this poor slave an opportunity to make up for his past failings."

Trish had recovered enough to think seriously about his proposal, but she could see no downside to letting him try. After he eased the car into the garage of the house they used to share, he came around to open her door and offered her his hand. She swung her legs out and let him pull her to her feet. He followed her to the house door, then reached around to open it for her. When they entered, she flipped on the kitchen light and he dropped to his knees.

"Thank you so very much, Ma'am, for this opportunity to serve you." He planted a kiss on the top of each foot.

She smiled. "I don't allow slaves to wear clothing in my house."

"Yes, Ma'am. Thank you, Ma'am." He rose and removed his shirt, hanging it over the back of one of the bar stools at the kitchen counter. She left him to finish undressing and headed toward the bedroom, pulling the blinds and curtains closed as she went.

He arrived in the bedroom moments after she did, naked, crawling on his knees. When he entered the door, he knelt, sat back on his heels, and placed his hands, palms up, on his thighs. She admired the thick muscles of his thighs and arms, his strong pecs, and the rock hard cock sticking straight up. She retrieved a dog collar that she'd purchased for play parties from her toy bag and buckled it around his neck.

"Thank you so very much, Ma'am. How may I serve you?"

"Undress me and give me a bath." She pointed to a bottle of bath salts on her dressing table. "You can use that."

"Yes, Ma'am. Thank you, Ma'am." He took the bottle into the bathroom and she heard the water running. He emerged and, still on his knees, unbuttoned her blouse, eased it off her shoulders, and hung it over the back of the chair. "Ma'am, if I may be so bold. I've very much missed how excited she gets when I played with her breasts. Perhaps Ma'am would allow me the privilege of licking them for her while the tub fills?"

Who could turn down an offer like that? "You may."

He reached behind her, unhooked her bra, and carefully releasing her double Ds so they didn't flop down hard on her chest. Without moving, he swung the bra so it landed on top of her blouse and his face melted into a big smile. Putting a hand under each boob, he licked one nipple and teased the other with his thumb. She moaned. He sucked on first one and then the other until she had to sit down on the bed because her knees had turned to rubber.

"The tub should be full now, Ma'am." He removed her sandals and unzipped her skirt. When she walked towards the bathroom, he slipped it and her panties down so she could walk out of them. He followed into the bathroom and knelt beside the tub while she stepped into it and lower herself into the hot, silky, rose-scented water. Brian reached for the Dove bar and slithered soap slicked hands over her skin.

He caressed her neck, then slowly worked his way down her breasts to her belly. Trish enjoyed the fact that she'd never felt a need to hide it from him. From there, he moved to first one leg and then the other, ravishing her feet with his strong, soap slippery fingers. He reached under her to wash her ass and her back, and then each arm, stroking down to her fingers. When he returned to her breasts, the look of reverence in his eyes when he washed them was a turn on in itself. Trish looked longingly at the swollen cock still pointing at her. She yearned to feel it inside her once again.

With her toes, she pushed the tub stopper up and used the sides to pull herself to her feet. Brian turned the water on and removed the shower head from its bracket. He rinsed the soap from her skin, turned off the water, and wrapped her in a thick towel. When he had patted her dry, she led him back to the bedroom.

"Boy, get my paddle out of that bag." She pointed to the leather case next to the bed.

"Yes, Ma'am. Thank you, Ma'am."

He handed her the heavy piece of lacquered oak. She flopped onto her back, grabbed his hair, and pulled him between her legs. His cock slid into her like it was finding its way home. She sighed with pleasure and then she reached around and swatted his ass with her paddle. He looked startled, but he didn't miss a stroke. Trish moaned. His cock massaged her inside and each time she smacked the gorgeous globes of his ass with her paddle, she got even more turned on.

They matched each other's rhythm, each of his thrusts followed by the strike of her paddle. Trish came hard, and then she came again. She was on the verge of a third orgasm when Brian begged, "Please, Ma'am. So intense. Can't hold out. I'm begging you, may I please come."

She was tempted to make him stop, to deny him. But she was so close. She hit him again, harder. "You may come, boy." Thrust, strike, thrust, strike, thrust, strike and they both cried out and exploded. Trish held Brian in her arms until he stopped trembling, then used his hair to pull his head up so she could look into his eyes. His pupils were wide and he looked a little out of it.

"You've pleased me, boy, but you've made a horrid mess. Clean it up."

"Yes, Ma'am. Thank you, Ma'am." He caressed her neck with is lips and paused to cover her breasts in kisses. Then he drew his tongue across her belly until he reached the cleft between her legs. He worked his way from the outside in, licking and sucking up all his own spunk. He finished by tonguing her clit until she came again with a shudder.

She tugged on his hair and pulled him into her arms. He lay beside her, his head on her shoulder, the leather of the collar smooth against her skin. She kissed him on the forehead. Every inch of her skin resonated with contentment. His breathing became deep and regular and her eyes grew heavy. Tomorrow, she would start training him to serve her outside the bedroom as well.

To Serve

By I.G. Frederick

Ryan stepped inside the restaurant, the heat billowing up to cloud his cold glasses with steam. Blinded, he brushed the snow off his parka, pulled down the zipper, and wiped his glasses clean on his cotton shirttail, then tucked back inside his jeans. He blushed when he settled them back on his nose and realized the woman who had e-mailed him her picture two days before stared at him from a padded bench along the wall.

She didn't look nearly as authoritarian as she came across in the dozens of e-mails they had exchanged over the past three weeks. The woman rose to her feet and picked up a leather coat from the bench. Memories of a dozen professional sessions assaulted him, but the diminutive brunette had promised him a different experience entirely.

"Hello, Ryan." She spoke softly, then turned to the stand where a buxom redhead consulted a seating chart.

"Table for two?"

The woman nodded and followed the redhead between

the rows of booths to one near the back. She took the seat facing the entrance and Ryan slid into the one across from her. A busboy placed glasses of water next to the paper napkins holding eating utensils.

"Did you have any trouble finding this place?"

He swallowed and reached for his water. He couldn't believe such a simple question rattled him, but his hands trembled when he lifted the glass to his lips so he shook his head rather than speaking.

The waitress stopped by and the woman ordered a glass of Merlot. Both looked at Ryan.

"I'll have a diet, please." When the waitress left he added, "Sorry I'm so nervous."

She smiled and he noticed green and gold flecks in her dark brown eyes. "I'm used to it." She kicked off her ankle-high boots and pulled her jeans-clad legs up onto the seat, crossing them on the vinyl in front of her. He realized the wide bench seats might prove uncomfortable to someone with such short legs.

"How long have you been married?" She captured a stray strand of her shoulder-length, dark brown hair and tucked it back behind her left ear.

"Almost ten years." He took another mouthful of water. "I'm committed to staying married."

She smiled. "I know. I respect that. You mentioned that you tried to introduce your wife to the lifestyle. How did she respond?"

He shrugged, but the memory of the grimace replacing Cynthia's normally inscrutable expression when he suggested they bring a little kink into the bedroom made him shudder. His wife's command of her world, her imperious attitude, had attracted him from the start. But it had never turned into the type of relationship he yearned for.

The woman across the table frowned, the sparkle in her eyes dimmed. "If I had a thousand dollars for every submissive male I've corresponded with who has spent time trapped in a vanilla relationship, tortured because he loves her but can't get what he needs from her," she shrugged her shoulders, "I could retire."

"I suppose there's some comfort in knowing I'm not alone." Ryan turned the wedding band around on his finger. "I do love her."

A woman in black slacks and a white blouse set his soda and her glass of wine on the table. Ryan looked up but couldn't remember if the rather stout brunette had taken their drink requests or not. "You two decided?"

"Yes," the woman across from him said.

Ryan grabbed the menu. "Go ahead, I'm sure I'll be ready by the time you're done." He skimmed the categories and found the list of salads. Although hungry, he knew he functioned better on a not-too-full stomach. "I'll have the chicken Caesar," he told the waitress.

The server left and Ryan turned his attention back to the woman across from him. She twirled the wine glass stem between her thumb and three slender fingers that each boasted a silver ring in various Celtic designs. "When did you realize you were a submissive?"

"I've always found very strong, assertive women attractive." He shrugged. "I don't know why."

She laughed. "Personally, I think that orientation is hard-wired at a fairly young age. I can remember incidents from when I was a child..." She lowered her voice. "But our society puts almost as much stigma on dominant women as it does on submissive men."

"I know." He sucked diet cola through the straw. "I have all these needs, and they're considered unacceptable for a man."

She took a sip from her wine glass. "Tell me about some of them."

Ryan tried to explain the urges that had driven him to this meeting, but he found it difficult to put into them words. Their food arrived, and she led the conversation down more mundane paths. To his surprise, she'd ordered a bacon burger with fries and she ate it all. He wondered how someone so tiny could consume such a large meal. By the time he'd finished the last bits of dressing-coated lettuce, Ryan discovered his hands no longer shook and he felt at ease. *Impressive*, he thought.

The waitress left the check in the middle. He reached for it tentatively. "I'm allowed to pay?"

She smiled and nodded.

He checked the total, stuck two twenties in the folder, and set it back down.

"I'm willing to take you home and allow you to serve for an afternoon. That will give you the opportunity to understand the difference between lifestyle and professional domination. It also will give you a taste of real servitude, help you determine if you're just someone who likes kinky sex or are a service submissive."

He lowered his eyes. "Thank you, Ma'am," he whispered.

She pulled on her boots, slid out of the booth, stood up, and handed him her coat. He held it while she slipped her arms in the sleeves and then settled it onto her shoulder. She pulled a long cashmere scarf out of the pocket, wrapped it around her neck, over her head, and around her neck again. He grabbed his parka and followed her through the restaurant stuffing his arms in the sleeves and trying to get the zipper to line up. She paused to button her coat and pull on leather gloves. When she approached the door, her hand did not reach for it and Ryan jumped to open it.

"Where are you parked?"

He pointed to his blue Dodge Ram.

"I'm in the red RAV4. You can follow me." She stepped through the half-inch layer of snow that had accumulated in the parking lot and Ryan wondered if he should have gone with her to open her car door. Then he asked himself what made him willing to follow her home, given the expectations she had detailed in her e-mails. He sloshed through the cold, his sneakers getting wetter, and climbed into his truck. When she turned left out of the parking lot, he followed.

A couple of miles and several turns later, she pulled into the garage of a one-story white house with dark blue trim on a small lot in a suburban neighborhood. Ryan parked in the driveway, swallowed hard, and climbed out of his truck. He followed her through the garage into a small entry with a coat hooks on one wall, and the entrance to a bathroom on the other. Ryan dropped to his knees and pressed his lips to the cold, wet leather encasing her feet.

"Thank you, Mistress, for allowing me to serve you."

"I'm not your Mistress, boy. Reserve that title for your wife if she'll allow it." She lifted one foot and he removed the boot, replacing it with one of the down, pink booties he found on the floor under the coats. He set the boot on the plastic mat next to the slippers and did the same for her other foot.

"You may hang your clothing there." She lifted a rattan cane with a suede-covered handle that hung from its black leather loop on one of the coat hooks. When Ryan had stripped naked, she turned her back on him and allowed him to remove her coat. "That goes in there." She pointed to a door next to the coat rack that opened into a small closet.

"Thank you, Ma'am." Ryan removed a hanger, carefully adjusted the coat, and hung it from the rod. He returned to his knees and waited.

"This way." Despite the pink slippers, she seemed sexier to him than any of the professionals he had paid hundreds of dollars to visit in their spiked heels and leather corsets. She walked through a living area, furnished in teak with brass accents and pointed with the cane to another door. "Cleaning supplies are in there."

The first couple of times she laid the cane across his ass, Ryan flinched, but he couldn't help enjoying the sting. She used it if he forgot to kiss her feet to ask permission to speak, or neglected any of the other protocols for behavior she'd required him to memorize, or if he missed something in the cleaning regimen that she explained before he started on each room. If he did anything contradictory to her instructions, she landed another stroke. Gradually, Ryan came to dread the sound of the cane whistling through the air. He scrambled to do each task exactly as she instructed, making sure he stayed on his knees, and avoiding eye contact.

By the time he returned the mops, dust rags, and vacuum to the closet, a sheen of sweat covered Ryan and red marks crisscrossed his back and rear. He washed up, then crawled into the living room and knelt in front of the sofa where she sat, curled up in the corner, a book in her hands.

"You didn't do badly for your first time." She unfolded her legs and stuck her feet in his face. She had removed the slippers and he admired the long, painted toes and slender arch. "Now that you've had the opportunity to serve in a life-style setting, how do you feel about it?"

Ryan kissed the ball of her right foot and massaged from heel to toes with his thumbs. "Some things I liked. Others, not so much."

She smiled. "When you attempted to introduce your wife to the lifestyle, did you try to get her interested in kinky sex, or did you discuss the dynamics of a Dominant/submissive relationship?"

He bowed over her foot. "I brought up the idea of kinky sex," he whispered.

"I have two problems with professionals. First, they aren't dominant. Men give them money and they give men what they want. How is that dominant? Who's in control?"

Ryan didn't dare look up to see her expression, but her voice had a disdainful edge to it.

"Second, they give men the false idea that the lifestyle is about kinky sex. That can be part of it. But more important is the devotion a submissive shows his Dominant. You'd be much better off taking a course in sensual massage techniques and introducing her to body, foot, and oral worship. Show her that she can have total control over you." She pulled her right foot away from him and proffered her left one for his attention.

Ryan showed her left foot the same care he had administered to her right. "You're right, Ma'am. She would enjoy that very much. And I think she might get off on the kind of control you exhibited today."

"People forget that BDSM stands for D/s as well as B&D and S&M. You can build a relationship on domination and submission. But, bondage and discipline, sadism and masochism are just play when you have time and if you have inclination. The first is a way of life, the others can spice up that life, but you don't need them."

○♂

Ryan unfolded the massage table he'd acquired on Craig's List and stretched a clean sheet across the padded leather. He'd made lasagna for dinner, Cynthia's favorite, and strawberry shortcake for dessert. He suggested she indulge in a bubble bath while he washed the dishes, but she'd used the time to catch up on some paperwork. She strode into the bedroom just after he filled the bathroom sink with hot water to warm up the massage oil.

"What in the world is this?"

Ryan swallowed hard then dropped to his knees in front of his wife. "I don't pamper you nearly enough." He kissed the back of one hand and then the other. "I need to put more effort into making you happy. Would you like to try it out?"

Cynthia shrugged. "Why not." She let him help her remove the sweats she'd changed into when she arrived home and stretched naked on her belly. He piled her long, black hair on top of her head and secured it with a large clip. Unable to resist, Ryan planted a soft kiss on the middle of each luscious mound of her ass before retrieving the oil. He poured a little into his hands and rubbed it into her shoulders. She gave a contented sigh. He could feel the tension in her muscles and worked to rub it away.

Thirty minutes later his hands and fingers had kneaded every muscle in her back, arms, and legs and Cynthia's skin glistened with oil. Ryan knelt near her face. "Would you like to turn over?"

She opened one eye. "I'm not sure I want you rubbing my front that hard."

"Of course not." He had to bite his lip to keep the word Mistress from emerging, but he so very much wanted to call her that.

When Cynthia rolled onto her back, Ryan switched his concentration from easing tension to arousing desire. He started with her feet, kissing her toes while he massaged the balls and heels. Then he worked his way up her legs, across her belly, stroking her skin with oil slick hands. When he reached her breasts, he first licked both nipples to attention, teasing them with his teeth the way she liked. He rubbed oil into the soft skin until she moaned and her hips rose slightly off the table.

Ryan took this as his cue and kissed his way from her breasts across her rounded stomach to between her legs. They opened to admit him and he inhaled deeply. His efforts had taken her just where he had hoped, and he put his tongue and lips to work to finish the job.

"Mmmmm. I don't know what's gotten into you, but I like it."

Encouraged, he licked her moist flesh, and pushed his tongue into her opening. His tool jutted straight out, but as the Lady had explained, this was about Cynthia. Ryan reached up to caress her breasts, and tweak her sensitive nipples with his thumbs. She gushed and he sighed happily, licking up everything he could. That set up a bit of a challenge -- the more he licked, the more honey flowed from inside her. He covered her hole with his mouth and sucked, massaging her clit with his nose. She pushed her hips upward, her breathing ragged and fast. Ryan released one soft breast and pressed his thumb against her nub while keeping his lips locked inside hers.

Cynthia moaned and her head turned from side to side until she exploded in his mouth. Ryan licked up all her juices and wondered if he could make her come again. But, she grabbed his hair and pulled his face out from between her legs. He whimpered a little, but didn't resist. He liked the feeling of her fingers tugging at his hair.

"What's going on?" Fortunately, she didn't look angry. Her pupils had expanded, almost hiding the green of her irises, and her eyes were only half open.

He swallowed. "I made a mistake, a few months back, when I suggested you consider kinky sex."

She frowned and released his hair.

Before she could speak, he dropped to his knees next to the table. "I should have explained that what I want is to serve your every whim. I want you to take control of me, of my life, of our marriage. I wouldn't mind kink if it's what you want, I think I'm a bit of a masochist. But that's for you to decide."

She rolled over on her side so she could look into his eyes. Her pupils had shrunk to normal, but her face still looked much more relaxed than when she had stretched across the table. "Exactly what are you talking about?"

"Do you know what BDSM is?"

She scowled.

"Bondage and discipline, domination and submission, and sadism and masochism. I'm mostly interested in domination and submission."

The eyebrows relaxed al little, easing her grimace just a bit.

"I would like to be your slave. To serve you. To give you complete control over my life. If you should decide you want to explore bondage and discipline or sadism and masochism, of course, I would participate. But, it's completely optional. If you don't think that's something you want to try, that's fine with me. I just beg you to consider allowing me to serve you, to call you Mistress when we're alone, to wear a collar as a symbol of your ownership."

Her eyebrows pulled together again, but her lips were no longer pursed so her expression was more puzzled than angry. He smiled. "I met a very lovely Lady last week, who helped me understand that I've approached this all wrong."

He rested his chin on his chest. This next bit would be the most difficult, but he needed to come clean. He inhaled deeply, steeling himself. "For the past two years, I've eaten peanut butter for lunch and saved up so I could visit professional dominatrixes." Her breathing told him that he'd aroused her anger and he quickly continued. "I never had any sexual contact with anyone, I promise. Mostly they'd make me crawl around on my knees naked and spank or cane me, just enough to hurt, not enough to leave marks."

He swallowed, afraid to look up and face the fire he knew he would find in her eyes. "But last week, I spent a couple of hours with a real Lady, a FemDom, someone men serve if she allows, who makes the decisions about what they get to do and how. She opened my eyes."

He peeked up at her face through his eyelashes. She wasn't happy, but she wasn't as angry as he had expected, either. "You're the only woman I've ever loved, Cynthia. But, I'm wired to serve. I need to submit."

"Did you get turned on when you visited these hookers?"

He nodded. "They don't consider themselves sex workers. I was never allowed to come. And I never served them in any sexual way so I've never gotten anywhere near as turned on as I got tonight."

She shifted so she could look over the edge of the table. "You're still hard."

"Yes, Mistress." He whispered the word, holding his breath. But, she didn't react. "Being on my knees, naked in front of my Goddess, is very arousing."

"And what are you going to do about that?" She pointed at it and it responded as if she'd touched it.

"Only whatever Mistress allows."

She raised one eyebrow and stared at him for what seemed like twenty minutes. "You've gotten me off. And, I'm kind of tired. I think I'll get ready for bed and go to sleep."

"Yes, Mistress. What would you have your slave do while you're getting ready for bed?"

She looked surprised and her eyebrow rose even higher. "My slave. Mmmm. I think I like the sound of that. You can go fold the laundry."

"Yes, Mistress. Thank you Mistress." He crawled out of the room and realized that she was testing him. He smiled. This test he would pass.

When Ryan finished putting the clothes away, he found Cynthia, wearing a bright pink cotton night shirt, propped up in bed, reading a novel. He knelt next to the bed, his hands resting on his thighs, his chin on his chest. He was still hard and while his body longed for release, a part of him enjoyed the agony of not knowing if or when Cynthia would allow it. She flipped the pages three times before she looked him up and down. "Go brush your teeth, slave."

"Yes, Mistress, thank you Mistress."

When he returned, she marked her place and set the book on the bedside table. "Turn off the light and get into bed, slave." Her voice carried no emotion, no clue as to her reaction.

But, she'd called him slave. He shivered with delight. "Yes, Mistress. Thank you very much, Mistress." He turned off the wall switch, crawled around, and climbed into his side of the bed.

Cynthia rolled onto her side, her back to him, and scooted closer. He turned toward her and ran his hand lightly up her hip to lay his arm across her waist. She pushed back against him, her ass pressing against his erection, and took a deep breath. He could almost hear her thinking. Then she turned to face him, pushed him on his back, and threw one leg over his hips. She pulled up her night shirt enough to free her pussy and sat on his cock. His eyes widened and he gasped.

"I believe we've established that you only get to come if I give you permission?" She tilted her head to one side.

"Yes, Mistress."

"I have no intention of doing so." She leaned forward, resting her hands on either side of his shoulders, and eased her hips up and down, riding his cock.

Ryan bit his lip, grateful for the orgasm control training he'd received as part of his prodomme sessions. Cynthia's eyes closed and her breathing grew ragged. She moved faster and he reached under her shirt to play with her breasts. That sent her over and she screamed and shook, dropping onto his chest. Her moist heat enveloped his cock and he pressed his fingernails into his palms to maintain control. When she rolled off of him, he both missed the contact and was grateful he had succeeded in serving her needs without coming himself.

She lay with her back pressed against his side and he turned so he could hold her, his rod pressed against her crack.

She sighed in contentment. "We'll have to talk about this slave idea more tomorrow."

Ryan smiled. "Yes, Mistress. Thank you, Mistress. I love you so very, very much." The last thing he heard before he slipped into slumber was Cynthia's deep, regular breathing.

Change in View

By I.G. Frederick

Rachel gave up trying to get a straight line. She threw the eye liner pencil in the trash and washed the mess off her face, settling on enough shadow, mascara, and lipstick to appear as if she had made up her face. Blessed with porcelain skin, as the bodice-rippers called it, she almost never wore cosmetics. But, for the gala she would have felt naked without some paint.

With two hours to get to the art museum, she entered La Crêperie and found Luke in one of the wrought iron chairs, his broad torso overwhelming the delicate, Naugahyde-covered seats. His green eyes practically bulged out of his head and he seemed to have lost his way with words, stuttering in his attempt to get any out.

"You ... Fuck ... Wow ... Stunning. ... " He stared at her from her light brown hair twisted up in a French chignon held in place with a rhinestone clip, to the low-cut, tit-hugging bodice of her little black dress, to its skirt that only came halfway between her thighs and her knees, to her four-inch spiked heels.

Rachel lowered herself into the chair opposite him. After

she was seated, he jumped up to pull it out for her.

Before either could speak, a curly-headed blonde bounced up to the table with a pad and pencil. "You two must be going to the gala."

Rachel smiled. Luke was wearing his usual leather jacket over black tee and jeans, nothing she would want to see on an escort for this evening.

"What can I get you? Our special today is a chocolate-filled crêpe topped with fresh strawberries and whipped cream."

"That sounds perfect." She would want to sample the elegant hors d'oeuvres at the gala, but knew she might not have a chance given her boss' expectation that she glad hand those attending.

"Yeah, sure, whatever." Luke's eyes never left Rachel's cleavage. Normally they met after work and she never bothered changing out of the tee shirt and jeans that she wore on days she didn't have to travel downtown to the office.

"Ma'am, can I ask you a personal question?" Luke had his hands in his lap and dragged his eyes away from her tits to look at them.

"I guess."

The waitress placed two plates piped with chocolate sauce, the promised fresh strawberries spilling across the filled crêpes, on the tile of the table. When Rachel cut into her crêpe with a fork, rich chocolate creme oozed out. She scooped together a bit of filling, wrapping, and berries and smiled when she closed her lips around her fork. The strawberries were almost as sweet as the cream and the chocolate was dark and rich.

Luke still had his hands in his lap. "You've been mentoring me for almost a year now. I've read every book you've suggested, taken all the classes you've recommended."

Rachel leaned forward and whispered. "You may eat, boy."

"Yes, Ma'am. Thank you, Ma'am." He picked up his fork and toyed with a strawberry. "Do you think I'm ready to serve a Mistress and let her train me to meet her specific needs?"

"If you find the right woman. That's why I suggested you

start attending the teas at the Center. You could meet someone there. It has happened." Not for her, unfortunately. She took another fork full from her crêpe and savored the berry-sweetened chocolate richness.

"What about you?"

Rachel set her fork down and dabbed at her lips with the napkin. "Me? Why? You've never expressed any interest before? We agreed on platonic from the beginning." She leaned toward him again. "If you're just looking for someone to beat your ass, you can try the pansexual parties. Lots of women are willing to play with men who aren't in service to them." Rachel had tried that. But, she hadn't had sex in so long, even just paddling someone turned her on to the point that she found it too painful to attend play parties.

"No. I don't think I'm really a masochist. I played with Bernadette and I didn't actually enjoy the pain. I'm keen on service. Making a sadistic Domina smile when she's abusing me -- that's the turn on." His whipped cream was melting and pooling on either side of his untouched crêpe.

She shook her head. "I don't follow..." Rachel took a deep breath and pressed her lips together to regain control. "Ah. Now, I understand. You know, I only get dressed up like this once or twice a year and then only if I can't get out of it." She tempered her disappointment with another bit of chocolate and fruit. "What you've seen so far -- jeans and tees -- that's me." She waved her hand past her chest. "This is just a façade I put on when I have to."

She extracted her cell from her clutch and checked the time. "I don't want to be late. Thanks for the crêpe."

He beat her to the door. "May I call you?"

"I think you've learned all I can teach you. Right now you need to train under the woman whose collar you want to earn so you can study how to meet her needs."

Rachel hurried across the street, as fast as she could balancing on the unfamiliar heels. She could feel his eyes on her rear and tried to man up her stride, but found that impossible while tilted forward by the spikes. Fortunately, the museum was only three blocks away and soon she was too busy thanking donors to worry about Luke.

♀

When she finally rolled out of bed at noon the next day, her feet still throbbing from hours tottering around on heels, she turned her phone on and found five text messages from Luke. She set the phone aside until she'd had her coffee and read the Sunday paper. The message notification pinged three more times and she ignored them all, composing the e-mail turning him down in her head.

On the fourth ping, Rachel opened her messages and shook her head. As she expected, Luke was begging her to train him so he could serve her. Each text listed another attribute he thought would appeal to her. If he had brought up the possibility anytime within the last eight months... She booted her computer and drafted an e-mail.

"Luke," she opted not to use "dear."

"You have to find a Mistress you think is beautiful when she's wearing sweat pants and a baggy tee shirt. She has to be beautiful to you before she puts on her makeup. Even if she's the type of woman who never leaves the house without putting on her face, you will be with her at home when she washes it off.

"Dominants can require their submissives to parade around however they please -- naked, dressed in lingerie and heels, wearing a French maid's uniform. But, submissives must adore their dominants however they chooses to present themselves -- whether that's stained boxers and unshaven cheeks or comfortable, baggy clothing with no makeup and mussed hair."

She paused wondering if she should let him know that she found his attitude offensive, but decided against it. He had seemed genuinely interested in learning how to serve. Still, if deep down he was a bottom in search of a woman to fulfill his fantasy, she saw no reason to waste any more of her time.

"I wish you the best of luck on your search. I hope you find the perfect Mistress."

She changed her signature five times before simply ending with "Lady Rachel." After rereading it twice, she sent it and turned off the computer. She changed out of her robe and headed for the park.

When Rachel logged in to work on Monday morning, she ignored the response from Luke until she clocked out. She had the mouse over his message, then decided dinner was a higher priority. Sue called while Rachel was stir frying some of the vegetables she had found at Saturday's Farmer's Market and invited herself over. Rachel appreciated the distraction. Luke's e-mail was still unopened in her inbox the next morning, buried under new messages and deadlines from work.

Rachel didn't open Luke's e-mail until three weeks later when she got on one of her periodic tears to clear out her cluttered inbox. She almost deleted it without reading it, but decided to at least see what he said. By now, he would have stopped expecting a response.

"Ma'am, you are correct and I apologize for not expressing my interest sooner. Throughout the months that you've graciously permitted me to learn from your wealth of experience, I've consistently had one thought: 'If I could only find a Mistress like Lady Rachel, I would be so very happy.'

"It just never occurred to me until I saw you last night that I didn't want to find someone like you, but that you were the one I want to serve. I beg you to forgive me for being so blind. I will understand if you don't believe I'm worthy of a response.

"I have until Friday to let my boss know if I'm willing to accept a promotion that requires I move back East. It's the kind of job that won't leave me any time to myself. If I can't serve you, perhaps that's for the best.

"Thank you, dear Lady Rachel for all your time and assistance. If I don't hear back from you, I hope you find someone more worthy of your collar.

"Your devoted servant, Luke."

Rachel stared at the words, stunned. When she'd first met Luke, Geoffrey was still, if half-heartedly, in her service. Luke seemed to have potential, but also suffered from many misconceptions common among those who learned about the lifestyle online. He'd been an apt pupil and she found him attractive. When Geoffrey was transferred to Dubai, she'd toyed with the idea of asking Luke to serve her. But, by then, their once-a-week dinner meetings had become routine and on the two occasions when she offered to allow him to accompany her to a play party, he'd claimed conflicting commitments. She shrugged. Not much point in answering now and causing him to regret accepting the promotion. Besides, if she had decided to train him and it hadn't worked out, he might have resented her for stymieing his career advancement.

♀

Rachel knew she wouldn't encounter anyone who had attended the gala at the erotic art festival, so she had no qualms about wearing the same dress. She chose a darker shade of eye shadow and a redder lipstick and skipped the pearl choker and studs. Rather than wear no jewelry, she added the gold chain earrings with dangling handcuffs Geoffrey had given her as a farewell gift.

While studying a painting of a woman in a full burka who was holding up the skirts to reveal she was naked underneath, Rachel heard a familiar voice whispering in her ear.

"I take it this is that other time of the year you get dressed up?" The words were barely audible over blaring heavy metal.

She whipped around to find Luke standing with his hands in the back pocket of his black jeans. He wore a leather vest which revealed his bare, muscular chest, leather chaps, and tooled black leather cowboy boots.

"At least this time I'm dressed appropriately enough to offer myself as your escort for the evening if you're interested." His smile looked sheepish and hopeful at the same time.

Rachel just stared at him.

"You look even more lovely than last time I saw you, if that's possible."

"Are you visiting to take in the festival?" She managed not to stammer.

Luke bowed his head. "I never left."

She blinked rapidly, trying to maintain her composure. "You turned down the promotion?"

At that moment, the music stopped and the DJ's announcements interrupted their conversation. Rachel weighed her curiosity about Luke's continued presence in Seattle against her desire to enjoy the festival exhibits, bask in the music, and watch the performance art. When the music started again, she moved to the next wall to look at a series of portraits showing women in shibari bondage.

Much to her surprise, most of the friends she encountered as she explored the galleries knew Luke as well. Eventually their two-some became a group of six with Ann, who had helped hang many of the paintings, sharing some of what she had learned as a volunteer. Together they watched the aerial artists perform, gasping as the women flew through the air. Finally they all collapsed around one of the tables near the back and sent the two males to the bar.

"I didn't realize you knew Luke?" Eleanor fanned herself with her program. "You haven't been to a FemDom event in at least a year."

"I'm the one who suggested he attend the teas." Rachel slipped of her heels and wiggled her weary toes.

Suzanne checked her makeup in a silver compact. "Well, I for one am glad you did. He provides excellent service and is fun to play with."

Mark and Luke returned and set glasses of wine in front

of Rachel, Eleanor, and Suzanne and a bottle of porter, dripping condensation, for Ann. Eleanor and Suzanne indicated the two empty chairs at the table. Mark took one, but Luke knelt at Rachel's feet.

"Ma'am, I noticed you've taken off your shoes. If your feet are hurting, perhaps you would permit me to massage them for you. Miss Eleanor and Lady Suzanne will vouch for my skills."

Suzanne raised one eyebrow over the other, but Eleanor giggled. "Oh, yes, he's very good. Indulge yourself. I'm just glad I wore my boots." She picked up her leather encased shins showing off the barely half-inch heels.

Rachel raised one foot in Luke's direction and he kissed the top before kneading her aching sole with his thumbs. Suzanne frowned until Mark eased out of his chair and positioned himself so he could reach her feet. She smiled and let him remove her high-heeled sandal. Rachel closed her eyes and let the heavy metal reverberate through her while Luke rubbed away the discomfort in first one and then the other foot. Ann and Suzanne had their heads together, but she couldn't hear their words over the music

Several songs later, Rachel opened one eye and noted that she and Luke were the only ones still at the table. She caught a glimpse of Suzanne and Mark gyrating with the rest of the dancers in front of the DJ station overlooking the event space. Luke's face was a study in concentration, his eyebrows drawn together, his eyes focused on her feet. His thumbs pressing into her flesh erased the tightness there while creating another wave of tension that settled between her thighs.

The bodies writhing on the dance floor were younger now, with more goth apparel and adornment apparent. Rachel checked her cell and was surprised to note it was almost two in the morning. She hadn't planned to stay for the after party. Slipping her free foot back into its shoe, she tugged until Luke released the other. He kissed the top again and replaced her second shoe. She extracted her cell and hit her speed dial for a taxi. Not surprisingly, she was put on hold.

Luke rose to his feet. "Ma'am, may I offer you a ride home? It may take a bit to get a cab."

She shrugged. At least she could find out what had kept Luke from moving back east. Accepting his proffered hand, she let him pull her to her feet and leaned on his arm as she tried to regain her equilibrium. When they finally emerged from the center out into the crisp night air, Rachel was steady on her feet again. She shivered, wishing she had thought to bring a coat. Luke wrapped the leather jacket he'd retrieved from the cloak room around her shoulders and she rewarded him with a smile.

"I'm just across, in the garage." She waited with him at the stoplight and found she was too tired to ask him questions. On the other side of the street, the click of her heels bounced off the walls of the almost-empty parking structure. He opened the door of a Mustang convertible and she sank into the passenger seat.

"You look kind of wiped out." Luke pulled his seatbelt on, turned the key in the ignition, and backed out of the spot. "Perhaps you'd like some breakfast?"

The thought of greasy hashbrowns and runny eggs made Rachel's stomach grumble and she realized she hadn't eaten all evening. She nodded.

"Hurricane?"

"Sure."

When they arrived, someone had selected Death Cab For Cutie's "I Will Follow You Into The Dark" on the jukebox. Luke led her past the red swivel stools at the counter and three guys in torn jeans and denim jackets watching a fourth knock balls across green felt. In the small back room, burning wood crackled in the fireplace along the back wall. He held out a vinyl-covered chair and she took a seat, feeling out of place among the bikers, drunks, tourists, and bar employees coming off shift.

A waiter with full tattoo sleeves, three facial piercings, and waist-length black hair in a thick braid down his back, dropped off two menus and plastic tumblers of water. He returned moments later with a coffee pot in each hand, one with an orange handle. Unwilling to forgo any hope of sleeping, Rachel held her cup in the direction of the decaf. She added cream and stirred slowly, finding herself uncharacteristically at a loss for words.

The waiter made it back to take their order before she could frame a question. When he'd disappeared again, Rachel looked at Luke and tilted her head.

"I couldn't leave." He sipped at his black coffee. "I know I had no reason to expect anything, but I couldn't abandon all hope of serving you. I decided to train myself as much as possible to be the type of submissive I thought you might want. I've taken classes in cooking, massage, and domestic duties. I've attended every FemDom tea since we last spoke, hoping I would see you there."

Rachel just stared at him. The waiter appeared again and set plates in front of them. Her eggs Benedict came with a huge side of hashbrowns. He had added fried eggs on top of a Typhoon, a massive portion of ham, green pepper, onions cheddar cheese, and tomatoes on a mound of hashbrowns. He scooped the sour cream and salsa on top and mixed it all together before diving in with gusto.

Rachel pierced one of her eggs and watched the yolk spill into the hashbrowns, joining the lemony hollandaise. She cut off a fork-full and enjoyed the combination of rich sauce, spicy sausage, the sulfur of egg yolk, and the grease of the potatoes. But, she still couldn't reconcile Luke's expressed desire to serve her, the effort he apparently had put into learning skills she could put to use, with the fact that he had never expressed any interest until he saw her in the dress she wore tonight.

Luke finally spoke after he'd plowed through almost two thirds of his breakfast including all four pieces of rye toast. At least he hadn't ordered seconds on hashbrowns. "I guess I was hungrier than I realized." He pointed his fork at her half empty plate. "Looks like erotic art's good for the appetite."

She shrugged and set down her fork, knowing she wouldn't be able to finish. "Why in the world would you pass up a promotion for..." she lifted her hands, palms facing the ceiling. She had never even responded to his offer to serve her.

He emptied his coffee mug. "I know. You never wrote back. For a while, I even tried to convince myself that my e-mail and texts had gotten lost in the ether." He shook his head at the waiter who held the coffee pot over his mug. "But, the more I thought about taking a job that would consume my life, that would allow me to forget about you..." he pulled a paper napkin from the chrome holder and wiped his lips. "I realized I didn't want to forget about you. You are everything a man could want in a Mistress: kind, intelligent, vivacious, beautiful."

Rachel swirled hash browns around in the sauce that spilled off her uneaten second egg.

He pushed his plate to one side of the table and leaned forward on his elbows. "I can imagine what it must seem like to you. You spend months sharing your knowledge and experience, and I don't mention a desire to serve you until you show up dressed to the nines."

The intensity of his gaze made her want to look away, but she found herself mesmerized by the brown flecks floating in the green of his irises.

"I beg you to remember, that when we started our relationship, you had a boy in service and I didn't know what I wanted. The truth is you're beautiful even when you're wearing your baggiest tee shirt and your loosest jeans and, frankly, I think you look better without makeup." He sighed. "I just was too focused on finding the 'right' Mistress," he lifted his fingers in quote marks and then put his hands in his lap "to realize she'd been sitting across from me every week for almost a year." He tilted his head, capturing her gaze. "What do I have to do to make up for my stupidity? Name it and it's yours."

Rachel couldn't remember the last time in her life a male had left her speechless. But, she had no clue how to react to his declaration. She set down her fork and closed her eyes, remember his strong fingers massaging the aches out of feet so very unaccustomed to wearing heels.

He leaned forward and whispered. "Ma'am, I've taken classes in skills I thought you might find useful, but I will take any others you wish. If you would like to sample my abilities, I would be happy to serve you in any capacity for any length of time, no strings attached."

Rachel rose to her feet and tottered past the now-empty pool tables. By the time she reached the entrance, Luke was there holding the door open for her while stuffing his wallet back into his jeans pocket. He held open his car door and when he put the car in gear, she gave him her address.

"Yes, Ma'am." she could barely hear the words over the engine, but their sadness permeated the car.

When they reached her building, Rachel spotted an open parking spot at least two blocks away. She knew she was too tired to walk that far. Luke pulled over to the curb, shut off the engine and turned to her. She raised one eyebrow and he pulled the emergency brake and scurried around to open the door.

Rachel pointed to the empty spot. "Park there. Number 532."

Luke's entire face lifted in a grin. "Yes, Ma'am. Thank you so very much, Ma'am."

She'd barely made it inside her apartment when the telephone rang. Leaving her door ajar, she punched in the code to unlock the lobby entrance, kicked off her shoes, and collapsed on the sofa. Glancing at the clock over the fireplace, she realized it was almost four and wondered if she should have waited until after she'd slept. But, her feet still hurt so.

The door closed and she heard the deadbolt click home and rustling in the front hall. After several minutes, Luke crawled into the living room, naked. He planted himself on his knees in front of her, his ass resting on his heels, his hands palm up on his thighs, head bowed, cock pointing straight up. For a moment Rachel admired his muscular physique, but her toes twitched. She pointed. "Feet."

"Yes, Ma'am. Thank you so much, Ma'am." Luke scooted into position at the foot of her red leather couch. He covered the tops of both feet in kisses, then gently took one into his long fingers. Although his expert ministrations sent thrills that chased up her legs to settle in her clit, they also eased away the tension that was the only thing keeping her awake.

⚓

When Rachel opened her eyes, bright sunlight crept across the beige carpet from the living room picture window and the rich smell of coffee emanated from the kitchen. She squinted at the clock. Noon. Pushing herself into a sitting position while rubbing her neck, she saw Luke on the other side of the granite counter, still naked at least from the waist up. The coffee pot beeped completion of the brew cycle and Luke emptied a ceramic mug, the water in it still steaming. He poured coffee into the mug and added cream. Balancing the cup on a small plate, he disappeared for a moment then emerged from the kitchen, knee walking until he was close enough to offer her the mug.

"Ma'am, I hope I wasn't too presumptuous sleeping on the floor near you so I could be available to serve you this afternoon. I thought perhaps if you invited me in, it was for more than to massage your feet until you fell asleep."

Rachel took a sip of the strong brew and blinked her eyes until she felt capable of speech. "I'm afraid I was too tired to think clearly last night."

Luke's smile drooped.

"But, I do want to give you an opportunity to show me how you could be of service."

The corners of his mouth bounced back up. "Thank you, Ma'am. I didn't prepare any food because I wasn't sure if you would want another breakfast or lunch. Which would you prefer?"

"Lunch. But, first, I need a shower."

"Ma'am, I would be delighted to prepare lunch while you

bathe. I took the liberty of freshening up in the bathroom off the hall so I wouldn't offend."

Rachel smiled. She could get used to this. She took another sip of the coffee. "You may finish this. I'll have a fresh cup with lunch."

"Yes, Ma'am, thank you, Ma'am."

In the shower, Rachel let the hot water run over her neck trying to unkink knots from sleeping on the sofa. Luke had said he studied massage, maybe he could rub them out. After drying off, she hesitated as she reached for a faded tee shirt and baggy sweat pants. She laughed, pulled them on, and stuck her feet into a pair of flip flops.

A single placemat with napkin and tableware was centered on one side of her cherry wood dining room table, in front of a chair facing the picture window with a view of the Sound. Luke dashed out of the kitchen to hold it for her and then zipped in and out bringing her a plate of crustless sandwiches with vegetable crudités and a small glass bowl of dip. Before she could settle her napkin in her lap, a steaming cup of coffee found its way to the placemat.

"Ma'am, I noticed you rubbing you neck earlier. May I massage it for you while you eat?"

She nodded and bit into one of the sandwiches. He'd combined leftover tuna with blue cheese crumbles, chopped celery, and mayonnaise for a delightfully piquant combination. His powerful fingers massaged away the tension in her neck and shoulders while she dipped a carrot stick in the bowl. His dip combined more crumbles with mayonnaise. She savored the combination of crispy vegetables, pungent cheese, sour bread, and fish.

"I must apologize for the Spartan fare, Ma'am. I didn't want to take the time to shop for something more presentable."

She took a sip of her coffee to avoid giggling. "This is lovely, boy." She closed her eyes, the tension in her neck quickly being replaced by a tightness lower down. Nothing was more erotic than a naked man devoting himself to her pleasure, and when she'd assuaged her appetite for food, other appetites began to emerge.

"What is your schedule like today?"

"I cancelled all my plans for the weekend while you were in the shower. I am at your disposal until I have to report for work Monday morning."

She knew her smile was smug, but she couldn't help herself. It had been so long since she'd had someone to play with. Finishing her coffee, she set down her empty mug. "You may take care of the dishes."

"Yes, Ma'am. Thank you, Ma'am." While he gathered up the crockery, she pushed herself away from the table and headed to the back room.

She flipped the switch which turned on a half dozen floor lamps to chase away the gloom created by heavy black drapes. The room had a St. Andrew's cross in one corner, a massage table in the other, a wall rack for her whips and floggers, and shelves for other toys. While she weighed which she would prefer to use on Luke, he crawled into the room and sat on his heels.

"Would, Ma'am like me to give her a full body massage?"

Rachel had been thinking of something more painful for Luke, but then she remembered he'd said he wasn't much of a masochist. Although the idea of him accepting pain only to please her was intriguing, she didn't think either of them were ready for that just yet. And the idea of his strong fingers doing for her back what they'd done for her shoulders and feet had definite appeal.

"You can turn the lights down a bit, you'll find a sheet for the table in that drawer there," she pointed to the chest next to the shelves, "and there's massage oil on the bottom shelf."

"Music?"

"There's some new age stuff in the collection." She nodded at the boom box and CD carousel on top of the chest then returned to her bathroom. After hanging all her clothing on the hook on the back of the door, she wrapped herself in the still slightly damp bath towel, and returned to the playroom.

In her absence, Luke had covered the table, put on an Enya CD, and dimmed the lights. He knelt beside the table, a bowl of water with a bottle of massage oil floating in it between his open thighs. He was still hard.

Rachel dropped the towel over his head and settled onto her stomach on the table, resting her head on her forearms. He hung the towel on an empty hook and poured massage oil into his hands. The scent of roses permeated the room and sturdy digits kneaded her back into a pliable pile of ribbons barely holding her skeleton together. As Luke rubbed oil into her back, shoulder, arm, and leg muscles, every part of her relaxed, except one. When he moved to her ass, the tension in her clit became overwhelming and her arousal overwhelmed that of the rose-scented oil.

She rolled over on her back and Luke reached for the bottle again. "I'm done with your hands, boy."

His eyes gleamed and he licked his lips. "Yes, Ma'am. Thank you, Ma'am."

Luke started with her toes kissing each one and then sucking all five at a time into his mouth. He licked his way up one leg and down the other, coming tantalizing close to where she really wanted his tongue. She wiggled her hips in frustration. Luke responded by switching to her fingers and sucking each one in turn. Then he kissed his way along one arm until he reached her nipple.

Only when each breast had been covered in kisses and every inch of skin licked, did he move his face down along the curve of her belly. Rachel moaned and pushed her hips up. Her skin tingled and her clit ached for his moist touch. When his mouth finally reached her mound, he gently pulled her lips apart and inhaled, smiling. Sticking his tongue out, he barely grazed her inner labia.

Unable to endure another moment of deprivation, Rachel grabbed his hair and shoved his face into her crotch. He opened his mouth and engulfed her nub with his lips, prodding it with his tongue until she exploded in his face.

He muttered, "yum," and kept lapping away until she came a second time.

Her clit too sensitive to take any more direct stimulation, she grabbed his hair and pulled his face up into view. He beamed, licking her juices off his lips. Rachel was torn between her desire to get even more intimate with him and her need for a nap. Her eyelids drooped. She was still tired from the previous night.

"Would Ma'am enjoy a siesta?"

She nodded and Luke scooped her up into his arms. She gasped, but he clasped her against his muscular chest and carried her to the bedroom. He held her over the bed so she could reach down and pull back the spread. Then he laid her gently on the satin sheet and covered her. "How would Ma'am like me to serve her while she naps? Cleaning, cooking, laundry, grocery shopping?"

Rolling over on her side and pulling the sheet over her shoulder, Rachel muttered, "You can do a load of laundry and make something for dinner."

"May I have permission to go to the market after I start the washing machine?"

She nodded and was vaguely aware of Luke uncovering her foot log enough to plant a kiss on it.

♡

Rachel woke to the smell of simmering garlic and onions wafting through the apartment. Her stomach grumbled and she looked at the clock, surprised to see it was almost six-thirty. She'd slept for nearly two hours.

When she emerged from her bedroom, she found Luke covered from neck to thighs with a full chef's apron, stirring the contents of a saucepan. He also had something cooking in her Dutch oven. A vegetable salad and a glass of white wine were waiting for her on the placemat. "Smells good." She took a sip from the glass, a delicate pinot gris with a fruity aroma, and tasted hints of honey and apple.

"I know you prefer red, but I needed white to cook with and thought as long as the bottle was open..." Luke took a plate from the oven and lifted strands of linguine from the larger pot with a spaghetti fork. When he raised the lid from the saucepan, the aroma of garlic, onion, butter, and white wine enveloped her and made her mouth water. He ladled some of that pot's contents over the linguine, set the plate on the table, and held out her chair.

Rachel sat down and took another whiff of the tantalizing scent wafting up from the plate. Scallops and shrimp swam in the sauce and when she wrapped her lips around a mouthful of pasta and seafood she closed her eyes to avoid distraction. "Wow. Apparently you had an excellent cooking teacher."

"I'm glad you like it. I took classes at the market tailored to taking advantage of the offerings there."

Rachel took a sip of wine. "In less than two hours you drove down to the market and whipped this up?"

Luke nodded. "I threw the laundry in the washer before I left and put it in the dryer when I got back. I'll fold it after I clean up the kitchen. The only thing I didn't have time to make was dessert, so I'm afraid you'll have to settle for chocolate mousse cake in ganache."

She laughed. "I'll suffer. I love Le Panier's cakes." She pointed to the plastic kitchen stool. "Fix yourself a plate so you can eat with me."

"Yes, Ma'am, thank you, Ma'am."

"I think it might be time for you to call me Mistress."

Luke stood staring at her for almost half a minute, his eyes wide his mouth half open. Then he dropped to his knees in front of her and covered her feet with kisses. "Oh, thank you so very much," he paused, "Mistress."

Rachel sighed, twirling her fork in her linguine. That word sounded so very good from his lips.

Acknowledgements

This book would not have reached your hands without the help of many dear friends and colleagues. I thank my readers and supporters, especially Cindy, my proofreader, editor, and best friend. Thanks also to all those who have served me, well and ill, over the years. I have learned something from each one of you and I hope that you find what you seek.

Other fiction
by I.G. Frederick includes:

Complicated Couplings
Four sexy stories about tangled twosomes

"If You Love Someone" — *Tara leaves her husband to move in with Nathan, but he abandons her after a few months. When he returns, begging her to take him back, life and love look very different.*

"Commiserate" — *The same man dumped them both. When they commiserate, they discover more in common than an ex-boyfriend.*

"Passion's Price" — *Richard steals Gina's heart from three thousand miles away. But, when he moves across the country, her intensity and passion for life drive him away.*

"Lunchtime Lover" — *Both married, they started their affair with the promise never to fall in love. Then Lisa's divorce becomes final.*

www.eroticawriter.net/ComplicatedCouplings.html

Cougar Conquests

Beautiful older women on the prowl and the sweet young cubs captured by their allure

"Benjamin" — *A chance meeting at a munch in a tiny town leads Benjamin to an opportunity for training. But, Lady Gina tries to end the relationship rather than emotionally torture herself.*

"Festival of Eros" — *The handsome young man followed her around all evening, behaving like the perfect submissive ... until she learned his identity.*

"Paddles" — *A biker bar with no bikers? The decor, name, and patrons of a bar in a small Eastern Oregon town puzzle William who just stopped in for a beer. Then the owner introduces him to the secrets of this very special tavern.*

"Starting Over" - *When her pet walked out on her, she stayed away from parties because it hurt to watch other women playing with their toys. But, a friend coerces her into attending a unique event.*

"The Cougar and the College Boys" — *Alone in the woods, hours from Portland, Tess discovers four college friends staying in a nearby cabin. The boys invite her to share their campfire, their dinner, and ...*

www.eroticawriter.net/CougarConquests.html

Dommemoir

WARNING:

This book changes women's attitudes about relationship dynamics, forever.

In Geneviéve's journey of discovery she dabbles in the BDSM lifestyle which forces her to recognize and acknowledge her true nature. Her memoir, woven together with that of a male slave, draws the reader into an intense odyssey of sexual expression triumphing over sexual repression while delivering fascinating insight about a different kind of love.

"The aptly titled Dommemoir *delivers on so many levels... It quickly sucks you in and envelopes you in the bondage of its spell...* Dommemoir *is a character study that breathes complex and compelling life into its hero, the devastating Lady Geneviéve and the fortunate submissives who worship at her feet... placing you in the delicious bondage of its dark and compelling landscape..."*

Larry Brooks, USA Today bestselling author of Darkness Bound **and** Bait and Switch

www.eroticawriter.net/Dommemoir.html

Eleanor & Mick

A journey of sexual exploration and insight

In five sizzling hot stories, Eleanor seeks refuge in a small town on the Oregon Coast and befriends her younger neighbor. He captures first her heart and then her submission, taking her on a journey of sexual exploration and insight.

"Salt for His Wounds" — When Eleanor's ex-husband shows up begging for a second chance, she asks her young, gorgeous next door neighbor for a favor and Mick takes advantage of the opportunity.

"The Mercantile" — Eleanor attributes Mick's detachment to the difference in their ages, but Mick confesses a need for kink. Afraid of losing him, Eleanor reluctantly consents to bondage and pain.

"The Things We Do for Love" — When her gorgeous girlfriend visits Eleanor on the coast, Mick's obvious attraction troubles her. But, Liz only has eyes for Eleanor.

"Paid in Full" — Mick's army buddy finds Eleanor hot and makes a deal with Mick. But, if Mick really loved Eleanor would he let another man have sex with her?

"Renovations" — After Mick spends a month renovating their garage, Eleanor discovers he built in a few surprises.

www.eroticawriter.net/EleanorMick.html

Family Dynamics

Six sultry stories exploring sexuality in Dominant/submissive liaisons

"'Aunt' Grace" — Jen needed a place to stay in Portland and turned to her father's stepsister. But, she found so much more than she ever dreamed possible with her "Aunt" Grace. Second Place, NLA:I John Preston Short Story Award.

"Leather Family" — Kyle needs his own boy. Jacques would do almost anything to find a place in a Leather Family. But, Kyle serves a female Master.

"Searching" — Two dominants love each other, but need someone who submits to them both. Just how far will young Jeremy go to serve the lovely Lady Theresa?

"Taking Control" — To free the woman she loves from a horrid sadist's perverted games, Melanie must set aside her own aversion to men.

"Family Ties" — When her slave's ex faces eviction, Katherine offers refuge. But can Naomi pay the price?

"Said the Unicorn" — Tessa dedicates herself to her Master's service, so his determination to add another woman to their family devastates her.

www.eroticawriter.net/FamilyDynamics.html

Fork In The Road:

**Changing people's lives, and relationships
in three pairs of sexy stories**

"Said the Unicorn" — *Tessa dedicates herself to her Master's service, so his determination to add another woman to their family devastates her.*

"Proposals" — *The evening appears perfectly arranged for him to pop the question. But, Christopher's proposition takes Geraldine on an unanticipated sexual adventure.*

"Winners & Losers" — *When he finally walks away from the blackjack table, Jeffrey finds someone worth gambling on.*

www.eroticawriter.net/ForkinRoad.html

Love Hurts
**but in a good way
five steamy stories about the dark side of love**

"B&D Trainee" — *Online, Xavier promised to make his B&D fantasies come true. But, had he jumped in over his head?*

"Knife Play" — *Seeking a knife he saw online, Jack*

inadvertently found himself in a room full of pain and bondage contraptions. He almost turned around and left, but a beautiful woman taught him a different way to appreciate blades.

"Pussy Whipped" — Eric knew nothing about BDSM, but purchased a ticket to a fundraiser to help out his friends. When Miranda asks him to "play," he discovers exactly what those four letters mean.

"The Auction" — He attended the auction with only one goal — to acquire a very special whip. But an offer to try it out proved irresistible and he discovered sometimes events, and women, can exceed one's expectations.

"FemDom Fairy Tale" — A FemDom's offhand remark about a photograph at an erotic art show draws a handsome man's attention. But, when two dominants find each other attractive, which one chooses to kneel?

www.eroticawriter.net/LoveHurts.html

Second Chances

Six sexy stories about getting a second shot at the gold ring.

"Back to School" — An admin error forces Jordan and Dennis to share a dorm room. Older than their classmates, they decide to stick together. But Jordan's past threatens to keep them apart.

"Gordon" — When the cover model of her latest book

walks into the coffee shop where she writes, Lenore embarrassingly calls him by her character's name. His reaction confounds her.

"Spa Date" — Dismayed that she introduced Sam to the woman who betrayed her, Julie tries to fix her up again.

"Salt for His Wounds" — When Eleanor's ex-husband shows up begging for a second chance, she asks her young, gorgeous next door neighbor for a favor. Mick takes advantage of the opportunity.

"Proposal — Tangled Webs" — The evening appears perfectly arranged for him to pop the question. But, Christopher's proposition takes Geraldine on an unanticipated sexual adventure.

"Starting Over" — When her pet walked out on her, she stayed away from parties because it hurt to watch other women playing with their toys. But, a friend coerces her into attending a unique event. (Condensed version originally published as "FemDom Party.")

www.eroticawriter.net/SecondChances.html

When Two's Not Enough
Seven sexy ménage stories

"Tribal Fusion" — Whenever and wherever he dances, Dominic collects propositions, but the Lady Lenore's proposal takes him by surprise.

"Two Brothers" — A divorcée in a flashy sports car attracts the attention of two young virgin brothers visiting the "big" city of Boise.

"Honeymoon" — Although she expected to honeymoon aboard a cruise ship, Allison finds herself sailing on a private yacht staffed by an incredibly beautiful couple. Believing her new husband wants to hide his older, less attractive wife, makes it difficult to enjoy the hedonistic delights offered in paradise.

"Jail Bait" — Serena wants Joshua to pop her cherry, but he won't touch her because of her age. When her birthday finally makes it legal, he arranges for a very special celebration.

"Nikki's Birthday" — Even someone happy in a monogamous relationship might find the gift of a hot, new toy for an evening of decadence incredibly exciting. (Inspired by a real birthday present given to a lovely little bi-sexual, genderqueer slave.)

"Market Boy" — When a beautiful Domme offers Jack the opportunity to serve at a party for her friends, he responds too quickly and too eagerly, getting more than he bargained for.

"The Cougar and the College Boys" — Alone in the woods, hours from Portland, Tess discovers four college friends staying in a nearby cabin. The boys invite her to share their campfire, their dinner, and ...

www.eroticawriter.net/TwoNotEnough.html

Young & Eager

Barely legal but hardly innocent

"Two Brothers" — *A divorcée in a flashy sports car attracts the attention of two young virgin brothers visiting the "big" city of Boise.*

"Teachers Pet" — *Trapped at an all-girls' school in the middle of nowhere, Sabrina tries to get her hunky teacher to bust her cherry.*

"Arresting Development" — *Bethany went out with Officer Rick to avoid a speeding ticket, but discovered she enjoyed getting "arrested."*

"Jail Bait" — *Serena wants Joshua to pop her cherry, but he won't touch her because of her age. When her birthday finally makes it legal, he arranges for a very special celebration.*

www.eroticawriter.net/YoungEager.html

Or visit
http://eroticawriter.net/
to find links to individual stories
and additional collections
and